by PARIS ROSENTHAL and JASON ROSENTHAL

Dear Boy,

illustrated by HOLLY HATAM

For the Rosenthal boys: Justin, Miles, and Ry. —P.R. and J.R.

Dearest Boy Linden, Thank you for being my inspiration for this book. —H.H.

HARPER
An Imprint of HarperCollinsPublishers

Dear Boy,

Believe in yourself
before others can believe in you.

Dear Boy,

Dear Boy,

It's okay if you don't run the fastest.

Just be the boy

who gives it

your all.

Dear Boy,

Play your favorite sport,

and be a good sport
while you're at it. . . .

Dear Boy,

It's okay not to know,

you know?

Dear Boy,

When you're alone with
your thoughts, you're never alone.

PETER PAN

A strange, blinking glow came from within
a water jug. Inside was a fairy, no bigger than your
hand. Her name was Tinker Bell, and she was in
the jug looking for Peter's shadow.

Peter appeared next. "Tink?" he called softly.

"Is my shadow in that jug?"

"No," Tink replied.

When Tinker Bell spoke, it sounded like bells.
It was a special fairy language known to Peter and
his boys.

Dear Boy,

Yes means yes.

Anything else means no.

Dear Boy,

Feeling cloudy?
It's okay to let the rain fall.

Dear Boy,

Know when to get dirty . . .

and when to clean up.

Dear Boy,

Find kids who
are like you.

Find kids who are unlike you.

Dear Boy,

Sometimes you may feel like
playing with trucks.

Sometimes you may feel like playing with dolls.

And other times you may feel like playing with both!

Dear Boy,

Note to self:

playing an instrument is a beautiful thing.

Dear Boy,

Honesty is one thing

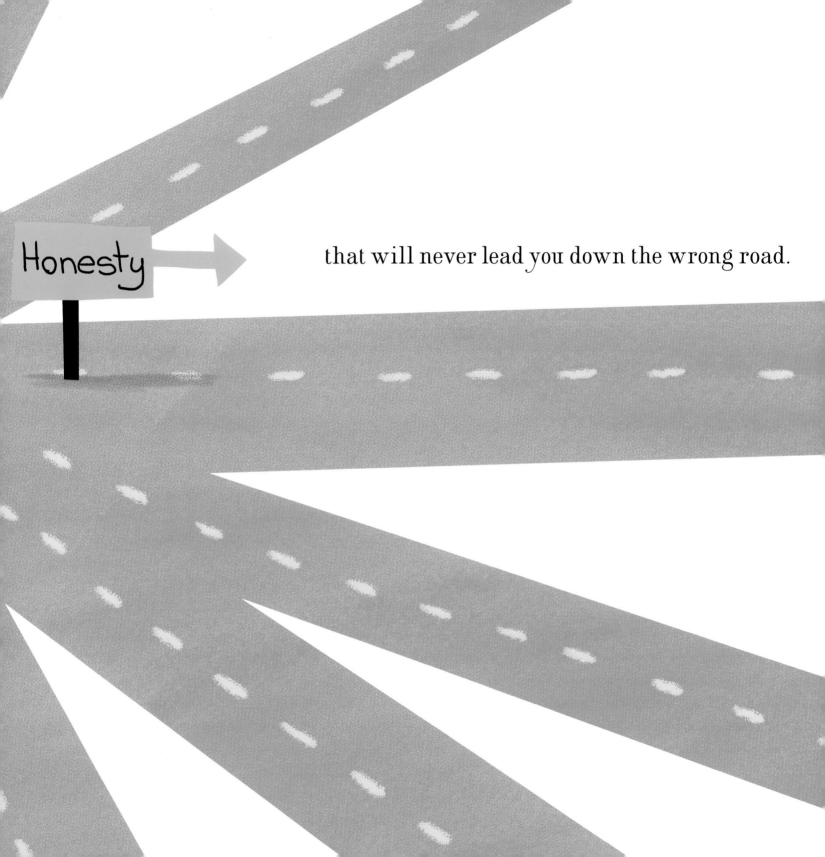

Honesty

that will never lead you down the wrong road.

Dear Boy,

If you need one more reminder to pursue your dreams, then here it is:

pursue your dreams!

Dear Boy,

Always trust magic.

Dear Boy,

If you can imagine it,

if you can see it,

you can be it!

Dear Boy,

Whenever you need an
encouraging boost, remember
you can turn to any page in
this book.

Most of all, dear boy
who I love, know that you can
always always always . . .

turn to me.

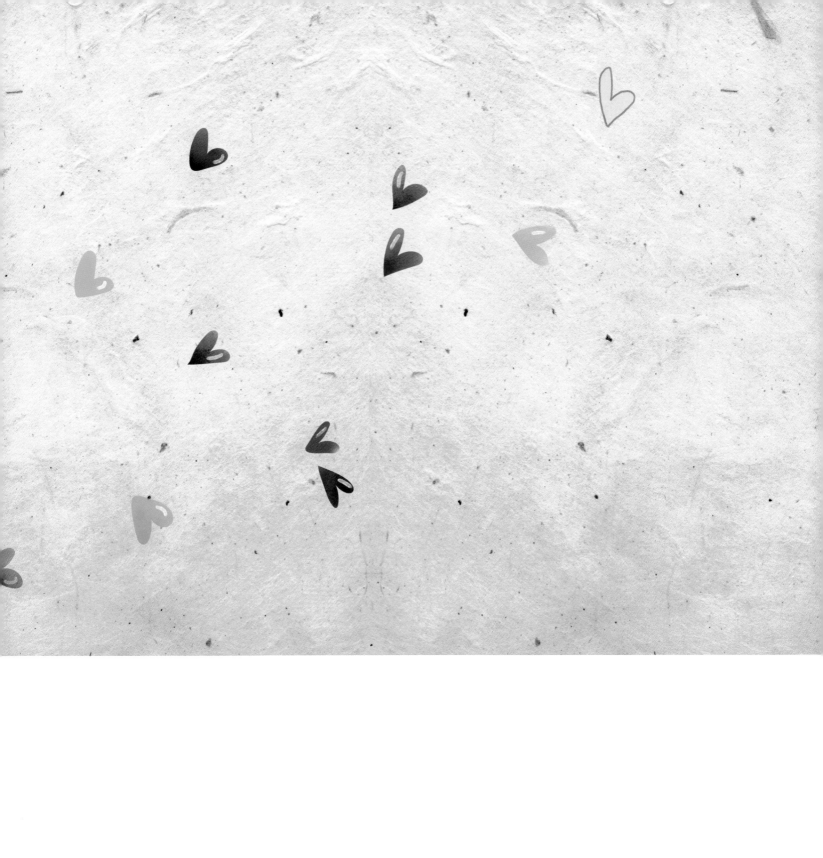